Bethan Woollvin

Rapunzel

TW🦉 HOOTS

Rapunzel lived all alone in a tall, dark tower.

She was trapped there by a witch, who visited every day.

"Rapunzel, Rapunzel, let down your hair!" called the witch. And then, using Rapunzel's hair as a rope, up she climbed, because that was the only way in to the tower.

Every day, the witch brushed
Rapunzel's hair, swish, swish.

Then

SNIP
SNIP

she stole some golden locks to sell for riches.

As she left with her treasure, the witch cackled,
"You can never escape, Rapunzel! Leave the tower,
and I will put a terrible curse on you!"

But was Rapunzel frightened? Oh no, not she!

If the witch could use her hair to get in,
Rapunzel could use it to get out.

So one day, she did.

After
climbing
down from
the tower,
Rapunzel pulled
her hair free,
and looked around.
Then she started
to explore.

The thought of returning
to the tower made her sad.
It's a shame about that witch,
she thought to herself.

So Rapunzel made a plan.
She worked on it secretly
every day.

And with the help of a new
friend she had made from
the forest, she was always
safely back in the tower
before the witch came.

The witch never suspected a thing.

Until one day . . .

"RAPUNZEL!"

The witch found a leaf in Rapunzel's hair.

But was Rapunzel frightened? Oh no, not she!
"The wind must have blown it in through
the window," she said boldly.

"Well remember," snarled the witch,
"If you ever leave the tower, I will put
a TERRIBLE curse on you."

And with that, she grabbed the end of Rapunzel's
hair and climbed out of the window.

But the witch
didn't get far before

Snip,
Snip,

she was sent
tumbling
to the ground.

The witch's cursing days were done.

So Rapunzel climbed out of the tower for the last time,
down into the forest where her friend was waiting.

And were the other witches frightened?
Oh yes indeed!

To my mischievous siblings
who inspire me, and fuel my
wicked sense of humour.

First published 2017 by Two Hoots
an imprint of Pan Macmillan
20 New Wharf Road, London N1 9RR.
Associated companies throughout the world
www.panmacmillan.com
ISBN: 978-1-5098-4267-4
Text and illustrations © Bethan Woollvin 2017
Moral rights asserted.

www.twohootsbooks.com